THE QUANTUM REALM
Philly the Photon

Mark A Montgomery

The Quantum Realm: Philly the Photon by Mark A Montgomery
©2015 by Mark A Montgomery. All rights reserved.
ISBN: 978-1-329-05715-9

All rights reserved. No part of this publication may be reproduced, distributed, or transmitted in any form or by any means, including photocopying, recording, or other electronic or mechanical methods, without the prior written permission of the author, except in the case of brief quotations embodied in critical reviews and certain other noncommercial uses permitted by copyright law.

Cover Design by: Daniel E. Montgomery
Scientific Consultant: Brandon Bentzley, Ph.D.
Editing by: Matthew Everett Jacobsen
Creative Consultants: Randy Reali, Matthew Everett Jacobsen

Facebook.com/PhillythePhoton

Contents

1. Ripping of the Sky 1
2. Unveiling the Path 3
3. Philly the Photon 9
4. Philly's Data Download 11
5. The Big Decision 15
6. Harnessing the Beast Within 17
7. Viki and Wiki 19
8. Relatively Speaking 23
9. Journey into the Electron Sea 27
10. Ellie the Electron 37
11. Negative Nancy the Electron 43
12. The Abyss of Emptiness 47
13. Grunk the Great Graviton 51
14. The Truth Seeker 55
15. A Path to Enlightenment 61
16. The Journey Home Begins 65
17. The Path to Light 67

Author Bio 73

Acknowledgements

Inspired by my son, dedicated to his existence in the space-time continuum. May this book forever stand as a monument of my love for him.

Becka, without your love and support, I would not exist. Thank you.

Dan, without you I could have never made this a reality. Your standard of quality has inspired me to do better. Thank you.

Matt S., your constant reflection and wisdom have both encouraged and challenged me to believe and grow. Thank you.

Randy, your creative contributions permeate the story. You're brilliant! Thank you.

Matt J., thank you for your collective contributions. Thank you for your belief.

Brandon, your level of intelligence is astounding. Thank you for your patience and scientific insight.

Thank you all for your friendship, love, support, belief in me and the impact that this book will have.

Introduction

Five years ago, I started a journey. With an inquisitive and curious nature, I pursued the underlying constructs of my own mind. This pursuit led to the exploration of Quantum Physics. What I discovered has forever changed my perspective on life.

The original manuscript was not targeted at adults to young adults, as this one is. However, this book is my heart and soul and indirectly reflects my own journey of self-discovery through the perspective of quantum patterns.

Philly the Photon is not written in a traditional formatted storyline where good confronts evil. If one truly wishes to understand their very nature of existence, then we must understand that the universe consists of the greys of relativity. Thus, I feel principle-bound to not promote absolute ideas of morality.

The children of our future need to understand four core concepts from as early as possible: 1) Shape, 2) Movement, 3) the Origins of shape and movement, and 4) Pattern Recognition as derived from the use of the Scientific Method. Ask questions, many of them, and expect answers that will lead to more questions and more answers. This is the formula for understanding life.

When we discover the formula that explains the cohesiveness of the entire universe, for indeed it is not simply a theory, but is an actual mathematical formula, then we will be able to replicate every level of complexity with precision. Our impossible will become our successive generation's plausible.

If we wish our children to delve into the sciences, we must make it relevant. Most of the time, this means creating an emotional connection. Emotional logic can lead to pseudoscience, but it remains grounded in some type of universal pattern. The Scientific Method can bridge the gap between Science and Pseudoscience when supplemented by an open mind from both perspectives.

I believe that *The Quantum Realm: Philly the Photon* will challenge you, educate you, inspire you, and increase your self-awareness and your external awareness. I hope that it incites you to look for the basic repeating patterns of the universe and apply them to your own life, in your relationships, and with your environment. It will increase your ability to think critically, rationally, and encourage you to ask more questions, yet find the balance between emotional and logical decision-making. Most importantly, this book will help you understand universal interconnectedness and of the impact that we have on everyone and everything in our environment.

I hope that you will enjoy the journey through *The Quantum Realm*. Let the adventure begin.

Chapter 1
RIPPING OF THE SKY

Lightning tore through the sky as if the fabric of the universe was being ripped to shreds. The expansive tendrils crookedly reached out to grasp tops of ancient trees. With tremendous violence, they were torn off in great explosions. The vast network of lightning seemed to span miles into the sky. Back and forth, the lightning went from sky to land, then land to sky in an amazing dance of power and colors.

The trail meandering through the woods was covered in shards, branches, and felled trees. It was nearly impossible to traverse. Thunder pounded the heavens as if great forces battled for supremacy. Fear rippled through the air on the currents of electricity to permeate their very souls. This was the substance of legends.

Running. Jumping. Climbing. Dodging. Taking momentary shelter. The storm had taken them by surprise and the boy was becoming paralyzed with fear.

"Listen to me, Sebastian! Look at me! We don't have time for you to be afraid; our lives are in danger. We must reach the house before the rain begins."

A freak electrical storm suddenly crept upon them, and what was supposed to be a two-hour afternoon hike around the beautiful Lake Chabot was being terminated abruptly.

He was fading in and out of focus. His father's voice sounded as if traveling through a tunnel at a far distance, then right next to him, then far away again. He was going into shock.

"Snap out of it! Come on, you can do this. Focus. Overcome your fear."

The trees were swaying in a roaring gust and a violent bolt of lightning touched down on an enormous Sequoia stump not more than twenty feet away. It erupted in flames, and chunks of glowing embers splashed on the ground while some erupted into the air as if it was responding with fury at its annihilation.

Sebastian was jolted back in a rush of emotion and adrenaline. The lightning continued to sizzle through the air in a hundred different directions.

What is happening? I've never seen anything like this. If the lightning strikes me, then I'm going to look like that stump. Where does the light come from? What is it? How does it simply appear, disappear, and have such power to destroy. I can't escape it. The lightning is everywhere.

"Sebastian, let's go." Emcie said in exasperation.

Why is he so afraid?

His father's face was furrowed with intensity as he held him by the shoulders and looked into his eyes with deep angst.

Sebastian understood, *we must escape the woods.*

They raced out of the forest. More than once, he felt as if he couldn't breath. The fear struggled to manipulate his mind and constrict his chest. He stumbled, tripped, and fell several times and he knew that his body would pay.

As they reached the car, he was exhausted. He ebbed and flowed between a state of fear and a need to understand what had happened. He'd never seen anything like this before.

I must understand what happened. I must understand.

Chapter 2
UNVEILING THE PATH

Sebastian sat on his bed, wrapped in a warm blanket. He looked out of the window into the maelstrom of lightning, rain, wind, and thunder. The storm had been raging for several hours now and it was late into the night. The lightning was less frequent and he anxiously anticipated the next brilliant bolt to crackle through the dark.

His father, Emcie, sat next to him in silence and looked out into the stormy night as well. A candle was lit on the nightstand next to the bed. It was swaying softly, gracefully, and was reflecting off the window.

Emcie thought about the lightning and thunderstorms he had experienced growing up in the Midwest.

I loved watching the lightning blast through the sky. I would count the seconds between the lightning strike and the moment that the thunder boomed. It would rumble through the heavens as it faded into the distance. I remember learning that the thunder is caused by lightning splitting the air apart and then slamming back together again.

It reminded him of powerful ocean waves pounding against the beaches. To this day, the rain would still soothingly coerce him to sleep as it pitter-pattered upon the roof.

He also remembered how his uncle, who lived down the street, would always come over before a storm. Many people were traumatized and afraid of storms and Emcie did not wish Sebastian to experience the fear he had on the trail every time a storm occurs.

A scratching sound startled him, but then Sebastian quickly jumped up and opened the door. Einstein tiredly looked up and yawned. He reached down and picked up his lifelong friend. Einstein was his little Jack Russell Terrier and always knew when he needed company. He returned to his spot on the bed and Einstein quickly curled up in his lap and snuggled.

Emcie looked towards the candle flame and stared at it for several moments. Eventually, Sebastian turned his gaze towards that soft, orange flame, too.

"How are you doing, son?"

Sebastian was mesmerized by the flame and his father's question pulled him out of his deep thoughts. "I'm okay. I feel a lot better now. I've never seen anything like that before. It scared me and I don't like being so afraid. However, it was so spectacular that I couldn't help thinking how similar it was to the magic wielded by some of the characters in the fantasy books that I read. Was that magic, Dad?"

"Sometimes legends and stories of magic are rooted in reality. No, lightning is not magic. There is a scientific explanation for it. Just as there is for almost everything, if not everything. Not so long ago, a bit over a thousand years or so, natural phenomena were still attributed to gods. Some believed that gods were warring against one another, or that humans were being punished for misdeeds and other fantastical explanations. We did not have the knowledge or understanding to accurately explain it at the time."

"That makes sense. I know that I could easily be tempted to imagine a fantastical reason for what happened today if I had no one to explain it to me."

"Really? Are there other things that you don't understand? Can you give me an example?"

Sebastian thought for a moment. "Like magnets, fire, and why I can't fly. I really want to fly, like a dragon. Can you imagine what that would feel like—to soar through the air?"

Emcie chuckled. "Yes, I have imagined it many times. There are many reasons why we cannot fly. The primary being related to something called gravity. Those are all great examples of how past generations have created magical explanations for what they saw and felt. However, they used more emotion than logic; thus, their information was inaccurate. They did not have the knowledge. Why do you think they didn't have the knowledge?"

"Because they didn't have anyone to teach them."

"Yes, that's true in part. However, if no one knows something, how does the knowledge come into existence at all? Is there some magical being that knows all? Does he or she whisper in your ear the complex explanations of the universe?"

Sebastian laughed. "No, I guess not, but I don't really know."

"How do I get you to think about something?"

"Hmm."

"Exactly. I ask you questions and you start to think about the subject. Asking how and why are the fundamentals of scientific thinking. Knowledge only comes by asking questions and then being open to whatever the truth may prove to be. You know that light helps us see, but why and how. Each answer produces another series of questions." Emcie paused and then asked, "Why does a light bulb work?"

"I only know it has something to do with electricity."

"What is electricity? What is *light?* Is the light from lightning, fire, lamplight, and the sun the same? What is heat? What is magnetism? Are heat and magnetism related? Is electricity related? Every level of understanding produces another series of questions. Every new bit of information has to be interpreted and it must fit into a larger puzzle. The interpretation of information is how differences in assumptions, ideas, and opinions originate. One's interpretation is always biased and is based upon already existing perspectives of what is truth. Being aware of how we are biased allows us to realize that other perspectives have merit too and can enhance the overall understanding of a given topic. Science demands that we repeat our experiments, duplicate the original observations, and then have others do the same. This process is called the Scientific Method. This has led to all the technological developments of our time. It is not a perfect process. However, as with other processes, I believe that it will be improved upon by some great scientist someday, maybe someone like you." Emcie looked down and smiled at his son. "This method and process reduces inaccurate assumptions better than anything else."

Sebastian smiled too. "Are all those things related?"

"Yes, everything is related, but we don't quite have it all figured out as of yet. Physics is the science that is seeking the answer. We are seeking the

Theory of Everything. The problem is that in order to find an answer we must first ask a question. The *key* is asking the right questions. This is not as easy as it seems."

"I don't understand. How do I know what is the *right* question?"

"Sebastian, there are so many things to learn, about ourselves and the universe. Sometimes it doesn't matter if we ask the right question. The point is to ask. However, at some point, we must ask the right questions if we want to achieve the next level of understanding."

"I want to understand lightning and its light?"

"The simple explanation is that it is electricity. However, there are several pieces of information that we must have in order to understand *what* it is, *how* it works, and *why* it exists. Do you know what is a photon? An electron? Gravity? Electromagnetic waves?"

"I've heard you talk about them, but I don't really understand."

"These are some of the fundamental truths of the universe that we must understand. These truths explain how everything is interconnected and everything works. Would you like to learn about some of these things?"

"Yes, I would very much, Dad."

"Good. Learning is a process though. I want you to start asking questions and trying to piece things together. Ask questions. You'll need to think critically and look for evidence to support your ideas and assumptions. It won't always be correct, but that's how gaining knowledge begins." Emcie paused as he thought about how to guide Sebastian.

"Start by asking yourself about light. What is it, where does it come from, and how does it travel from one point to another? Also, ask yourself about fear. Try to understand what is it and why it is such a powerful emotion. We'll talk about it tomorrow."

Emcie sat silently with Sebastian for several more moments. He loved watching the storm.

"Goodnight, son. Sleep well and feel better."

Emcie left and Sebastian lay in bed, snuggling with Einstein, and thought about how afraid he had been.

I can't allow fear to control me like that again. Dad always talks about 'having courage'. How does courage help me overcome fear?

He stared into the candlelight and pondered its existence.

What is light? It seems to come from so many sources. Is fire part of light? Does it come from the same source? What about lightning? Light bulbs? The Sun? Electricity? It seems like they are all related. How?

Sebastian lay awake for some time until the candle burned out and he fell into a deep sleep.

Chapter 3
PHILLY THE PHOTON

Zoom. Schweeeeezzz. Schwoooosha.

What's happening? Sebastian frantically thought as he realized he was in the midst of a very lucid dream.

He stared out into a vast darkness that reminded him of outer space. Small specks of light littered the darkness like the stars. *They are all moving. Wow, this is cool.*

Several of the tiny specks of bright white light were darting back and forth around him. They were moving rapidly and he was frozen in fear.

"What's happening?"

Zip, zing, zweeeeennng. One of the beautiful specks of pure white light appeared directly in front of Sebastian.

It was spinning very fast. The speck of light began to grow larger and larger as it slowed down until it was as large as a soccer ball. It was a perfect, ball-shaped sphere.

When it finally stopped spinning, it reflected all the colors of the rainbow in a dazzling display of light. It was similar to the colors that stream across the surface of a soap bubble except it glowed with a pure white light from within.

"It is marvelous!" he whispered in awe.

The sphere cast its bright light upon Sebastian. The light also revealed that he was floating within the vast darkness.

The rainbow of colors began swirling in pools, and then Sebastian realized that they were forming a face.

Sebastian bordered on being afraid, but he kept himself still as he watched it form.

The eyes were large and excited, darting here and there, assessing Sebastian. His mouth grew into a broad grin that conveyed mischief.

"Who are you? How'd you get here? I know! I know! No need to answer. Are you afraid? Ha! Yes, you are. Where are you from? I know! I know! You're a Zigbot from the planet Ziggy! I'm Philly, Philly the Photon! I'm a Light Particle, which is where I get my name—photon, a light particle, same thing. Welcome to the Quantum Realm!

Chapter 4
PHILLY'S DATA DOWNLOAD

"A *light* particle!"

Instantly, Sebastian remembered his thoughts right before he went to sleep.

I have so many questions that I need answered. I don't know who or what this creature is or whether it wants to hurt me, but I can't let my fears keep me from understanding him. I can try using courage to overcome my fears. Maybe if I expect something good to occur. This is my chance to experiment! I will be friendly and hope that he will be as well. I suspect that he will teach me about Light Particles. Hmm. I wonder if there are other types of particles.

"My name is Sebastian! My Dad was just suggesting that I try to understand light. I want to know everything! I want to understand what a... photon, did you say? Yeah, what is a Photon? I want to know about light particles. Are there other types of particles? What exactly is a particle?" Sebastian was so excited that he couldn't stop talking.

Then, with a burst of light and a fast spin, Philly interrupted in a roaring, high-pitched laughter. Sebastian realized that he was mimicking Philly's excited manner and instantly erupted in laughter as well.

"Okay, okay, Sebastian." Philly began slightly less franticly, "Well, hmm, how to explain this. I am a light particle. In the Quantum Realm, a *particle* describes a very, very, very, verrrrrrry small object. What is the smallest thing you can see?"

"Sometimes I see little specks of dust floating through the air."

"Good example. Now imagine something fifty billion times smaller—that's a particle in the Quantum Realm."

"I can't imagine something that small. How do we measure things in Quantum?"

"Well, we have special ways to measure size and distance down here. We do not use miles or kilometers and feet or meters. One way that we measure is the Planck Scale, which helps us measure the effects of gravitational attraction over distance. It was named after one of the fathers of Quantum Physics, Max Planck. Yes, yes, we'll have you *walk the Planck*." Philly chuckled, but he knew that Sebastian would not be laughing when the time came for him to dive into the abyss.

"Do particles have shape? Like balls or squares?"

"That's a good question. Yes, they are spheres. However, some things can only be measured by how they affect their surroundings. These are referred to as forces. There are four fundamental forces: electromagnetism, the nuclear forces—the strong and the weak force, and gravity. Forces create and combine with particles to make larger and larger *patterns*. Would you like to know the sequence of patterns that give rise to life?"

"Sure, Philly. I have a million questions."

Philly smiled. "Of course you do. That's a smart boy. Here we go. The nuclear forces are simply called the strong and the weak force. They attract specific particles together to form a nucleus. Then the electromagnetic force forms around the nucleus and can attract or create other specific particles called *electrons*. Electrons orbit around the nucleus and form layer after layer. The nucleus, orbiting electrons, and the electromagnetic force form atoms. The Table of Elements lists all the different atoms. Hydrogen, Oxygen, Helium, Carbon, Sodium, Iron, and Uranium are just some of the different types of atoms. Different combinations of atoms create molecules. Molecules combine with more molecules to eventually form cells. Cells combine with other cells to form increasingly complex structures. These structures range from single-celled organisms to bacteria, plants, animals, planets, stars, etc. Gravity's strength increases with the size of the structures and keeps everything connected.

"That sounds like the same patterns repeating over and over."

"Yes, yes. Human intelligence is a direct result of the ability to recognize patterns. Good job. Your body has evolved to recognize, interpret, and organize shapes, sizes, colors, smells, feelings, sensations, and movements into *patterns*. The entire universe is formed from these repeating patterns. The universe is comprised of these repeating patterns and explains it from a single particle to the largest galaxy."

Philly looked at Sebastian and thought it might be time for some fun. "Come on, Sebastian, let's play tag!"

Chapter 5
THE BIG DECISION

Sebastian and Philly spent quite a while laughing and playing. Philly showed Sebastian how to utilize his mind for controlling gravity in order to move in any direction he wanted. This led to an awesome game of tag. Sebastian was getting good, so Philly thought it was time to see if he was ready to start their adventure.

"Are you ready? Are you ready, Freddie?" Philly playfully tried to rhyme.

"Ready? Ready for what?"

"What is *light*, Sebastian?"

"It's a particle."

"Yes, yes, of course; but how do particles come into existence? Why there are different colors of light? How does light travel?"

"I don't know, Philly. You didn't give me that information."

"Yes, yes. That is correct, I did not. We must go on a journey, a great adventure to discover this knowledge. Only when you have reached the Lair of Grunk the Great Graviton will you have the answers."

"Uhh, I'm not sure I like this idea. This, umm, Great Grunk sounds horrible!"

"Grunk is powerful and wise, and he will demand a price for his knowledge. I will guide you through the layers of Quantum and we will need the help of my friends. Indeed, my friends will help us. The journey to the Lair of Grunk the Great Graviton is fraught with danger. You must prove worthy to enter his lair or you will never find it and you will never return home."

"Philly, this has been a lot of fun and all, but I'm not sure that I want to go. Who am I? I'm nobody! I don't do dangerous things. I barely made it out of the woods during the lightning storm. Yeah, I don't think I can or want to go on this journey." He was very afraid and doubted his ability to make it back home.

"It is your choice, your choice alone. If you choose to go home and wake up, you will never have this opportunity again. You may however, choose to face your fears. I encourage you to embrace your fear with courage. Come and gain the knowledge that very few have been given the chance to discover. If you choose to believe in yourself, then you will never regret your decision, regardless of what may come. I believe in you. Yes, yes, Sebastian, and so does your father."

Sebastian had not considered what his father might think.

Does he believe in me? Would he approve of me doing this? Oh man, I just don't know if I have what it takes.

Sebastian contemplated it in silence for some time. He looked around in the mysterious Quantum Realm and imagined what else could possibly be out there. He was afraid—of the unknown.

There it is again, he recognized, *that fear of what I don't know. I don't understand why I have to risk everything, but I do know that I'm tired of being afraid. I guess this is my chance. Dad suggested that I use courage to overcome my fears, too. Well, let me give it a try.*

All right, I'm not going to let my fear keep me from obtaining the knowledge that I want. I'm going to expect an amazing adventure. I must believe in myself and that I can do this, that I will become worthy to enter Grunk's lair, and that I will find my way home again. I think that Dad will be very proud of me then.

Sebastian closed his eyes, recognized the fear in his belly, and gathered all the courage he could.

"Let's do this, Philly. I'll do my best!"

Philly looked at him with admiration. A big cheerful and proud smile sparkled across his face in a beautiful spectacle of colors.

This boy is going to achieve great things.

Sebastian's heart sank to his stomach as Philly snatched him along without warning. They moved, oh boy did they move, through space and time, at the speed of light—at the speed of Philly the Photon—the amazing light particle!

Chapter 6
HARNESSING THE BEAST WITHIN

"PHILLY! Waaaaaaaaaaait!"

Sebastian was so scared. His face was rippling and he felt sick to his stomach.

"Have courage, Sebastian. We must reach the outer realms of the Quantum Layers before we are safe. Yes, yes, the Layers of Quantum! Focus, Sebastian! Control yourself. Control your fear and turn it into strength! Now come on. We must hurry."

Sebastian was on the verge of screaming. *Focus? How am I supposed to focus? There is so, much, pain.*

Nevertheless, he did. Through the pain and in a surge of inner strength, Sebastian willed himself to focus. He reached deep within, visualized a black tube surrounding his spine, and breathed. Deeply. Slowly.

He imagined it sucking the fear from his mind, then his heart, and finally, from his belly into the tube. In a state of intense focus, he sent the fear erupting out from the top of his head.

It spewed forth and at that moment, he realized something life changing. He could harness his fear, and possibly other emotions as well, to give him strength of mind and will. With that *self-awareness*, Sebastian attained peace within and control over his fear.

He opened his eyes and looked at Philly.

Wow! I am flying through space like a soaring dragon. If only Dad could see me now.

Sebastian felt the rush that came with his courage and embraced the newfound confidence.

With a single thought of intent, he steadily moved towards Philly until he was directly across from him and then tried to surge forward thinking to outpace him.

Philly laughed as he realized what Sebastian was attempting. "You can never outrun me. Nothing can move faster than the speed of light."

Sebastian playfully gave him the evil eye, but he wondered why. *This is too much fun. I'll just save that question for another time.*

Philly sensed Sebastian's moment of growth. He knew that he would have enough strength and courage to see this difficult journey through to the end. It would demand more from him, but he had learned how to tap into the source of the universe, the great sea of glue that connects everything—gravity. He would need this knowledge to prove himself worthy of the Master of Gravity—Grunk the Great Graviton.

He is strong, very strong. Yes, yes, but it requires a lot of practice to maintain that level of focus. Yes, I must hurry.

Philly drew Sebastian closer to him, set his intent, and dug deep within himself too.

Focus. No more games. I must find the fastest way for Sebastian's sake.

They were moving at 186,000 miles per second—the speed of light.

Indeed, Sebastian was losing his focus. The pain was beginning to burst through his head, pounding his skull. It was as if a troll was trapped and viciously beating the walls of his prison. It was vibrating down his neck, into his chest and Sebastian was on the verge of passing out.

Vhroooom. In a flash, all the pain ceased and he drifted off into a deep sleep, safe in the outer realms of the Quantum Layers.

Chapter 7
VIKI AND WIKI

Sebastian was slowly waking. His eyes were still closed, but he could hear Philly's quick, erratic and playful voice whispering.

His eyes burst open and he looked around.

"Where am I?" Sebastian asked softly. This was a weird place. Nothing was linear—in a straight line. When he located Philly and his friend, it was not in a direct line of sight. It was as if his line of sight traveled along a curve, also known as an *arc*. Sebastian imagined a basketball traveling along an arc as it was flying toward the hoop. He saw things as if they flowed along the path of that arc and was unable to see straight ahead. It was very disorienting at first.

The air looked as if it was vibrating too. He recalled his trip to the Grand Canyon. The desert floor radiated heat into the air, and it made the air appear to be vibrating. This looked the same except without any heat.

I wonder if this is how a fish sees in the water.

As he looked around, he realized that he was in a large glass-like bubble. The outside glowed bright neon blue. It was breathtaking.

"Hello, Sebastian," someone greeted him with a very melodic thought.

What is this?

Sebastian turned his head over one shoulder and then another looking for the source.

I don't hear her voice, but I hear her. How is that possible?

"Sebastian, meet my friend. This is Viki the Vibration," Philly introduced.

Sebastian was in awe as he met the gaze of this wonderful being.

Viki was beautiful! She stood upright, and her body was shaped like a thin towel that rippled up and down like an ocean wave. She moved so gracefully.

"She's so beautiful!" Sebastian mumbled slowly as he tried to keep from staring.

Philly started laughing hysterically. "He is smitten, Viki! He is smitten indeed!"

"You're a long way from home, young Sebastian!" Viki soothingly wrapped him with her melodic vibrations.

He realized that she was not speaking as he would. Instead, she was gracefully rippling her body, which radiated subtle flashes of various colored light.

I understand her.

"Amazing," he mumbled aloud.

"I am a *vibration*, Sebastian. I speak in all the different vibrational *frequencies*. I flow like the ripples across water from the drop of a pebble. My vibrations flow along in waves across the universe."

"How is it that I can understand you?" Sebastian instantly realized that he was not speaking with his mouth, yet she understood him.

Sebastian also realized that every time they moved or communicated, the air-like substance around them rippled in all directions like pulsating waves.

"You can understand my vibrations because *you* are nothing more than a system of vibrations. What do you think your *senses* are? How do you see, smell, feel, touch, taste, or hear? What is it that you are sensing?"

Sebastian did not respond for a time. He began looking around and noticed how vibrations were being sent from all the different beings and objects. Each one had a unique ripple pattern that flowed into the space surrounding them.

"Viki, what exactly is a vibration?"

"A vibration is derived from movement. A particle or force moving in one direction interacts with another particle or force moving in an opposite or different direction, creating a moment in which the movement patterns of both are disrupted. The disruption causes a ripple-like effect to occur in all directions. This is a vibration. These specific types of ripple patterns are called frequencies."

He analyzed the environment again. When two or more separate sets of vibrations interacted, they seemed to create a new pattern of shape, size and directional flow. They created various geometric shapes. Some vibrations bumped into one another and then came back to him in a different combination. Others appeared to have many different vibrations merging to form very complex geometry. These formed long channels through the space.

Then he understood.

"When the vibrations interact, some of them come back to me. When they reach me, I see flashes of color take shape in my mind, hear something new, and feel the changes on my skin. Are my senses receiving information from these vibrational patterns?" Sebastian asked.

"Yes. Vibrations rise and fall as they flow. These peaks and valleys are considered *waves*. We call the different types of waves *electromagnetic radiation*. The waves can have different *heights* and *widths* between the *peaks* and *valleys*. The distance from one peak to the next is its *wavelength*. The shorter the wavelength is the higher the *frequency*. The longer the wavelength is the lower the frequency. The distance between each peak and valley is its *amplitude*. Every frequency can have different amplitudes. This means that the same frequency wave can be relatively large or small."

"Hmm." Sebastian tried to summarize this scientific idea, "So, vibrations are moments of opposing movement. This movement travels in waves that can have measurable patterns called frequencies. Frequencies can vary in height between the high points and the low points, and can vary in distance between each peak. The height refers to its amplitude and the width refers to its wavelength. The number of wavelengths in a given measurement of time or distance is its specific wave frequency. Vibrations refer to a series of these moments of interaction; or rather, vibrations are a series of different wave frequencies interacting. I guess some of the waves move faster than others too."

"Actually, all waves move at the same speed—the speed of light. However, the wave itself moves continuously at the same speed." Viki knew this was difficult for him, but he was doing well.

"WuOOFaa! WuOOFaa!"

All of sudden something that resembled a dog came rippling out from another room. It looked like a long hot dog, but it had the same wave-like shape as Viki except it kept changing the frequency and amplitude of its wave as it moved. It also emitted ripples of various colors of light, just like Viki. The wavy hot dog was very adorable and raced over to Sebastian expecting to get attention.

Sebastian looked at Viki and asked, "Is it ok? It won't bite me, will it?"

Viki laughed and responded, "This is my companion. His name is Wiki, Wiki the Wave, and no, he will not bite you. Although, he may try to lick your face."

Everyone began laughing, and Sebastian reached down and petted the fantastic little wave.

"Will he be going with us?" Sebastian asked with excitement.

"Yes. Wiki will help show us the path through the raging Electron Sea. You must learn to work with him as I do."

"Oh, this is getting fun again! You and I are going to be good buddies!" Sebastian said as Wiki began wiggling up and down trying to lick him.

Viki and Philly looked at Sebastian with fondness and allowed him to be happy in that moment. Sebastian would be facing danger soon enough.

Chapter 8
RELATIVELY SPEAKING

Time was different in the Quantum Realm. Sebastian had no idea how long he had been here. He wondered whether his parents were worried about him or even if it had been longer than a single night. All he knew was that it seemed like days, perhaps weeks since he had begun his journey.

"How long have I been here, Philly?"

"Well, hmm. Yes, let's see how to explain time. Do you know what time is?"

"Sure, time is, time issss; well, I don't know what time is. I know that we use a clock to tell time. I think it has something to do with the earth spinning. Oh yeah, years are measured by how long it takes the earth to move around the Sun. Hmm. It seems like all we do is measure time. No, I don't know what time is. I never thought about it."

"That is a very good start. Time is only a measurement. What do you think we are measuring?"

"Well, years are measured by how long it takes the earth to move around the Sun. Minutes, hours, and seconds are measured by how long it takes the Earth to move or spin around one complete turn. So, maybe it measures movement."

"Good, good! Well done. That is only half of the equation though. In your world, time is measured based upon specific wave frequencies emitted from an atom. In general, how do we know something is actually moving?"

"Because I can see and feel it," Sebastian stated confidently.

"Hmm. No, not exactly. This question has been a debate among humans for a long, long time. If a tree falls in the woods, and no one hears or sees it fall, did it actually fall? How can we prove it? Yes, there are many opinions. Asking a question like this is called a *hypothetical* question and is considered a *thought experiment*. Albert Einstein was a renowned Scientist, a Physicist. Your dog Einstein was named after him. Professor Einstein was famous for conducting thought experiments. Do you know what I mean if I say something is *relative*? Yes, *relative*. Have you ever heard your Father use this term?"

Sebastian thought about this for a moment and then attempted to explain, "Relative. Oh, sure it's like someone who I am related too, right?"

"Haha, yes, yes, indeed. That is one definition for the word. However, your relatives are all related. Related to what? To whom? Think harder, Sebastian."

He attempted to remember if he had heard this term before in a different way. Then he remembered something his father says.

"Dad says it's all relative! It just depends on your surroundings. He refers to something called Relative Normalism. Yeah, that's it. He is working on a theory that he calls Relative Normalism. But I don't know what that means."

"Yes, yes," Philly chuckled. "Stand up for me. Now spin around," he instructed. "Now, how do you know that you actually moved?"

Sebastian looked around him. "Well, because when I spin, nothing around me moves, yet everything that I sense and see changes depending on the direction I am facing."

"Exactly! Yes, indeed that is it. Time is a measurement of the change in location or movement between two or more objects. Time doesn't exist without movement. At the beginning of the universe, nothing moved. With nothing moving in relation to something else, there is nothing to measure. Movement refers to what?" Philly posed.

"Vibrations?" Sebastian hesitantly responded.

"Correct! Movement begins at the particle level between two opposing frequency patterns. This is called *contrast*, like when you see my vibrations blending into your vibrations *relative* to one another. Contrast is the moment when two or more vibrations, flowing in different directions at different speeds, combine and change from two or more opposing patterns into a new single pattern. Contrast establishes a relative moment in time in which the direction of a wave or particle stops momentarily, relative to its environment, and then moves off in another direction. Time is a measurement of this movement. Yes, time: the change in movement between relative patterns or forces. We call this the *space-time continuum*. There is no way to measure time without movement within three-dimensional space. Now, gravity alters the progression of time in the space-time continuum. Ha, that is a difficult concept to grasp, huh, Sebastian," Philly realized. "Don't worry, you will understand the concept of *time* and *relativity* much better later on during our journey. Just remember: if there were no movement occurring within the universe, there would be nothing to measure, there would be no change occurring, and time would never exist."

He understood some of it, but it was still a bit confusing.

"For now, just realize that time on Earth progresses at a different rate than in the Quantum Realm."

Sebastian's brain felt like it was a grapefruit being squeezed as he tried to understand time. "I'm quite all right with letting that question go for now," he expressed with relief.

Chapter 9
JOURNEY INTO THE ELECTRON SEA

Sebastian awoke to a sudden rotation of the bubble. It was quite forceful and almost threw him and Wiki the Wave, which was curled up next to him, to the floor.

As he opened his eyes, he realized that the blue glow around the bubble was much brighter. The bubble was also vibrating much faster.

"Wooffaa! Wooffaa!"

"It's time, Sebastian," he felt Viki vibrate. "It's time for us to enter the Electron Sea. Come. You must learn how to guide Wiki and his wave."

Wiki jumped up into Viki's arms as a portal opening appeared in the glowing bubble. Sebastian noticed streams of blue light flowing away from the portal and into the distance beyond.

Slowly, Viki the Vibration started to vibrate. Then something spectacular was happening.

Wiki's hot dog-shaped body had grown in size tremendously and was flowing up and down continually. Wiki was vibrating the same frequency as Viki, but his amplitude was greater. He leaped through the portal and began digging a tunnel within the Electron Sea of blue light.

A few moments later, his head was about ten steps deep into the sea and there was room enough to walk behind him. Viki walked through first and maintained a focused state of mind.

Philly looked at Sebastian and said, "Are you ready? You must stay close and watch how Viki flows with Wiki. You will need to learn how to control your frequencies and focus your thoughts so that Wiki can understand what you want from him."

He looked at Philly the Photon and then stared into the tunnel that Wiki was creating in the enchanting sea of blue light particles. Sebastian felt the fear rapidly rise from his stomach to his throat and it made him cringe.

I must not fall prey to my fear again! I have the strength and courage to see this journey through. I have my friends to depend upon as well. Be strong and face your fears. I got this!

With his resolution, Sebastian stepped through the portal with Philly close behind.

"This wave tunnel is amazing!" he observed with curiosity. "The walls are moving. It's as if some of the electrons flow in opposite directions like little streams. I see little faces flowing back and forth. It's funny looking! It is difficult to tell whether we are moving or if the walls are and we are standing still."

Philly spun around slowly looking up, down and behind him. The tunnel was closing in on itself about ten steps behind. It seemed to be collapsing slightly slower than Wiki was digging.

"Sebastian, do you see what is happening behind us?"

Sebastian looked towards the rear, and as he did, he stopped moving forward. The closure started gaining on them, and he was startled for an instant then quickly spun around and caught back up with Viki and Wiki.

"I suppose that we need to stay close to Wiki, huh!" Sebastian stated matter-of-factly while laughing.

"Yes, yes, indeed! Do you understand what is happening?"

"Well, it looks like Wiki can wiggle in the same direction as the electrons are flowing. There are small streams of electrons flowing in opposite directions too."

"Yes, yes. Electrons are a quantum particle and are characterized by the direction of their spin: up spin—counter clockwise, or down spin—clockwise. All electrons are negatively charged, which means that they have an attractive force. However, they live in groups of either positive or negative charged clouds and form in layers around the nucleus of atoms or groups of atoms."

Sebastian remembered that it was important to ask questions to gain knowledge and understanding. "If all electrons have a negative charge, then what makes a cloud either positive or negative?"

"Great question. Well, electrons flow back and forth between these clouds. The direction is determined by what we consider a *net* change in the number of electrons between two clouds. If one cloud has more electrons flowing out than coming in, then it has a net outflow and its charge becomes positive. A positive charged cloud has a strong attractive force and it will attract electrons from its partner cloud. A negative charged cloud is full and has more electrons than it's partner. The partner clouds always desire to have a balance—an equal distribution of electrons. However, sometimes they are influenced by other areas outside of their cloud's boundaries. When this happens, a wave stream is formed due to the flowing of electrons from one cloud to another. An example of this occurs when lightning strikes a treetop. This movement of electrons in waves is an *electrical current.* Does that make sense?"

Sebastian tried to reason aloud what was occurring in the tunnel, "I think so. Wiki has a net positive charge and the Electron Sea has a net neutral charge. He will influence the directional flow of some of the electrons as he comes into contact due to the difference in charge. Why does the tunnel start collapsing though? Is it because we are moving forward?"

"Yes, yes. He only directly affects the change for as long as he maintains contact. He has the ability to conduct *electricity*—the flow of electrically charged particles. His temporary impact affects the entirety of the sea's movement and form forever, but the initial change in the shape, movement, and strength is not permanent. Electrons are always flowing in waves toward the positive charged areas. They are trying to regain their balance—net neutral."

"Philly, do humans impact our environment in the same way?"

"Yes, yes. All objects in the universe, from particles to planets and stars, have a net charge, or influence, on our surrounding environment. Both you and I affect our environment and are affected and influenced by our environment. Humans have a net positive or negative effect on their environment in a physical way, including their impact on other humans. Your vibrational pattern form systems within your body: heart, muscles, organs, and brain. These different vibrational systems combine to create a personal unique pattern of net impact that emits from you and have an immediate impact and influence on your environment. However, no action or impact is ever singular in nature. Every action creates a rippling effect in the overall system of vibrations forever in time. Do you understand what is a *ramification*?"

"I think so. A ramification is the delayed result of an action."

"Yes, yes. Correct. Every movement you make, every choice, thought, and word that you speak, is a result of someone's or something's vibrational patterns that have existed from the beginning of time. You are a ramification of the atoms that were created by, and came from the stars. It is a continuum of action and reaction, of changes and impacts of vibrational patterns, and is carried on highways of waves throughout time. Do you think that anyone has the ability to measure every ramification of their actions, either positive or negative, that they have on their environment?"

"How could we? Wouldn't that make us able to tell the future? No, that would be impossible."

"That is correct. However, there is a way to predict some of these ramifications of your actions, attitude, and words. Look at the tunnel and how Wiki is affecting his environment."

Sebastian looked at the walls again and the longer he looked the more he realized that there was a very *predictable* pattern.

"By observing people, the effects of your actions and words on others, the changes of the earth and sky, and even electron movements, you can learn to recognize the patterns. Learning to recognize patterns is at the core of intelligence. Once you learn a pattern, you can use that pattern as a tool to manipulate something, someone else, and yourself. This is called *awareness*. Applying this awareness to better understand yourself is called *self-awareness*. Everyone has different levels of awareness. There are a great many different patterns and some have greater awareness of specific patterns while others have greater awareness of other patterns. If I ask you to look at a painting from fifty feet away, what could you describe?"

"Not much. Maybe it's flat, it has some colors on it, and it's a certain size."

"What if I asked you to move along a circular perimeter by one-quarter, in which the painting is at the center? Would it look the same?"

"Hmm. Well, not if the painting was square and flat. I would only be able to see the side edges of the painting and I probably wouldn't even be able to tell that it is a painting."

"Yes, yes. How right you are. And if you rotated another quarter."

"I would see the back of whatever it is painted on. Perhaps a canvas stretched across a wooden frame. However, I wouldn't see any painting. Where are you going with this, Philly?"

"I could continue to ask you to describe this painting from several different vantage points, such as from the top, the bottom, etc. In fact, you can observe any moment in space and time from only one of 360 times 360, which totals 129,600 different vantage points. These are also referred to as *perspectives*. Anything that can be observed is a relative point in time and space in which it is the center sphere of perspectives. You, as an observer, can only observe from a single perspective at a given moment. Now add to this number of potential perspectives, the number you would have if you moved towards the object by twenty feet, then five feet, etc. Ignorance—the lack of knowledge is forever a part of the observer; it is impossible to observe all angles simultaneously, which is the only way to *know everything* and make one's opinion absolutely correct. However, who do you think would be able to describe the painting better: someone who has observed it from 360 different perspectives or someone who has observed it from only one perspective?"

"Duh. Someone who has seen it from 360 different perspectives."

"Exactly. Why?"

"Hmm. Well, I guess because I would be able to understand the pattern, the painting in this case, a little better with each new perspective. The more information I have to make assumptions, the more accurate my assumptions. Each new perspective would allow a deeper level of awareness." Sebastian finished his answer with a big smile from being able to reason through and understand the concepts of *perspective* and *awareness*.

"Well done. Yes, yes, well done. Humans have a history of assuming if they have a personal experience in which subsequently they develop a belief, then everyone else should come to the same conclusion. One can develop an opinion based upon limited information and limited observations and then presume to think that their assumptions are accurate. It is all right to believe in your ideas and assume their accuracy, but we must be open and willing to modify our assumptions when there is contradictory or complimentary information and perspectives."

Philly paused while he watched Sebastian contemplate in silence. After a few moments, he began speaking again.

"Life is based upon incomplete sets of information. The brain has the ability to fill in the holes of missing information with our preexisting assumptions. These assumptions are developed by the collective number of perspectives that one obtains from relative environments and experiences. Entire civilizations have been influenced by those who exert power and control over them to fear knowledge. Most people thought the world was flat for thousands of years. It is a good thing to have opinions and ideas, but it is not a good idea to presume that yours is always right. This is prideful and arrogant. It is ok to be wrong. It is ok to change what you think is true in the face of additional observations, experiences, and perspectives. Remember this Sebastian: the people who have the ability to see life from many different perspectives, and are not afraid or too prideful to embrace newly discovered truths, will always be the wisest. The more patterns that you recognize, and the more observations that you have of those patterns, the more accurate and wise your opinion, perspective, and understanding will be. Now, why is this important to understand?"

"Well," Sebastian began reasoning aloud, "pattern recognition can be used as a tool to manipulate other patterns, like how levers and gears can manipulate the objects that they move. Observing a pattern from multiple perspectives, although always incomplete, will increase the accuracy of my assumptions. If I am fearful of having my beliefs and assumptions proven wrong, then I will not be able to advance my level of understanding or attain deeper levels of awareness."

"Bingo! The Scientific Method is the best model for discovering new patterns that can be duplicated and used as tools for further exploration. Experiments and observations are at the core and can be applied to every aspect of your life. Now, what are patterns?"

"It is a system of vibrations, or wave frequency interactions, that occupy space and are in constant movement." Sebastian thought he was smart.

"Incomplete! You're missing something," Philly chided.

Sebastian was confused.

I know that vibrations travel on waves and they occupy space, but what else is required to make it a pattern?

"I don't know. What else makes a pattern?"

"It repeats. If a movement cannot be repeated, then it cannot be a pattern. We must be able to observe a series of occurrences, like a specific frequency wave, over and over again in order to recognize it as a pattern."

"Oh yeah. Got it!"

Sebastian looked up at the tunnel walls again. He saw the backward flowing electron waves and noticed how they were spread out in even distances from each other.

There is so much to learn. How am I ever going to earn Grunk's favor?

"Philly, it's awesome to learn how everything flows and works together throughout the universe, but it is also so much information and gets overwhelming at times."

"Ahh. Yes, yes, it can be. Well, Sebastian, have you ever heard of a *learning curve*?"

"Hmm, I don't think so."

"Well, let's see. Do you remember how difficult it was to learn how to play the guitar when you first started?"

"Ha! Yeah, I sure do. My fingers were always cramped on one hand and on the other my fingertips were always raw."

"How long did that last?"

"I guess after the first few months my hands stopped hurting and I could remember the positions without much effort."

"That's called a learning curve, Sebastian. It always takes much more effort to learn something in the beginning. The initial curve is really, really steep, like the upslope of a wave. Then you get over the hump, like the top of the wave, and everything you learn becomes much easier, like sliding down the slope of a wave. This is a normal cycle in life."

"So, all the things that I'm learning in Quantum will be challenging in the beginning, but it will get easier with time," he reasoned.

"Yes, exactly. Once you have an opportunity to apply what you have learned to everyday life, it will take less effort. Soon, you'll be able to recognize more and more patterns without all the effort."

"Well, I have a feeling I am going to forget a lot of what is happening."

"Indeed you will. It's normal. That is why understanding the *process* of asking questions and *thinking critically* is so important. Ask the questions yourself and you will find that remembering the answers is much easier. If you forget, then just ask the question again and you will find the answer again."

I sure hope so.

Viki turned to Sebastian and vibrated, "Are you ready to try this?"

He looked at this beautiful and graceful being and thought, *How am I going to figure out how to influence Wiki's wave?*

He was experiencing self-doubt and Viki understood.

Sebastian had already learned so much, and it was affecting his ability to focus. He had no choice though.

I must prove myself worthy, to myself and to my friends that have helped me so much.

"Come Sebastian. Move in front of me," Viki vibrated while Sebastian mustered his strength and moved forward.

"Now, quiet your mind. Place an image of Wiki in your thoughts and hold it, focus on it and don't think about anything else."

Sebastian's mind was racing. He was thinking about the moving walls, the electrons, his Mom and Dad, Grunk the Graviton, about Wiki. *Think about Wiki.*

Sebastian held the image and the emotions that he associated with Wiki. *He's such an adorable wave.* Finally, everything went still in his mind.

Viki softly vibrated the specific frequency towards Wiki. Sebastian saw it in his mind, felt it in his body, and began gently flowing in the same soft rhythm.

It's like listening to music that makes me dance. It just flows right through and makes me move, except now I see the wave frequency pattern in my mind.

"Now hold this frequency. Control yourself. Control your mind. Hold your focus and let everything else just float away." Viki's vibrations were very soothing.

Sebastian felt the strength surge through his body as his focus sharpened. His ability to flow with the vibrations became greater the more he *experienced* and flowed with the waves. He could see the vibrations in his mind as he felt the rhythmic flow.

Hmm, I wonder what will happen if I try to change the frequency.

That was all it took. In an instant, he felt Viki's last vibrations say, "NO! DON'T! Stay with Wiki, Sebastian! Focus his frequency. He will reflect you now."

With those last vibrations, Sebastian and Wiki were sucked away into a fast and turbulent sea of electrons. He lost his focus, his control, and he was barely able to hold onto Wiki as they were tossed about for what seemed like days.

Chapter 10
ELLIE THE ELECTRON

"I failed, Wiki! I failed!" Sebastian cried. They began to tumble around even more violently. "I can't control it. I can't focus, Wiki! Help us," he pleaded, but Wiki was actually having fun and was enjoying the current's flow.

Maybe if I just let go... and... stop... fighting.

Even as he thought it, Sebastian's body relaxed and his mind became quieter. Sebastian allowed himself to *sense* the movement of the electron waves, and both Wiki and Sebastian started flowing in a regular rhythmic way again.

Now I need to focus. I need to set my intent on finding a safe place and instruct Wiki to find it.

Sebastian regained control by, ironically, not resisting and letting go.

I'll need to think about that more when I'm safe.

He sent out a subtle frequency as he held the image of Wiki in his thoughts. Wiki instantly perked up and was at attention. His body began flowing in the same frequency that Sebastian visualized. The tunnel opened up quickly as Wiki began digging away.

Sebastian was exhausted and was barely capable of maintaining enough focus to send out the instructions, "Wiki, find us a place to rest."

Sebastian and Wiki started moving faster and faster. He was fading and once again, the strain ended abruptly. He stayed awake and aware long enough to sense his body float onto what felt like a soft cloud and to hear a sweet and excited young voice.

"Look what I found, Mom!"

Wiki had understood the instructions and had found refuge. Sebastian looked through half-closed eyes and saw that it was another bubble. This one was very large, and it radiated blue from within while it was dark outside.

A small blue sphere of light appeared with big white eyes. She was a bit larger than Philly, hovered above his head, and looked at him with a bright smile.

"I'm Ellie, Ellie the Electron. How ever did you get here! You're safe now though, yes, very safe. Momma and I will care for you. Sleep now human," Ellie spoke softly while trying to contain her excitement.

What an adorable creature, he thought as he fell into a deep sleep with Wiki curled up next to him.

Ellie fluttered around with excitement, but decided to let them sleep for a while. Quite some time had passed and she grew too impatient, so she decided they had slept enough.

"Hello, human! Hey. Get up. Come on. Come on." Sebastian was still trying to wake up, but Ellie was attempting to drag him and Wiki off to play.

Sebastian laughed.

"What's your name, human?"

"Sebastian."

"Well Sebastian, get up! Come on! Let's go play."

She is so cute, like a little bee buzzing back and forth. How can I resist?

Sebastian jumped out of bed and chased her down the street. All the electrons greeted Ellie. She was everyone's favorite.

"Hi, Ellie!"

"Slow down, Ellie!"

"Come have tea this afternoon, Ellie!"

On and on, all the way down the street, electrons were very happy to see her. Once they noticed the human following, they all began to chase after her.

"Wait up, Ellie! Who's your friend? Wait up!"

Ellie stopped and let everyone catch up.

"Here, have some tea, Ellie. Some for your friend too."

"Here, Ellie, have a charge," one of them playfully joked and proceeded to zap her.

She giggled. "Stop that Auntie!"

Sebastian thought a *charge* was like being tickled, and it made him laugh too.

Then they all turned their big white eyes towards Sebastian. Big smiles and happy faces looked at him in anticipation.

He seemed to be their center of attention. It was difficult to look at them individually because they all began circling. They appeared to be orbiting around him. Some formed an orbit that was closer than others. In each layer, the number increased. He also noticed that the different layers orbited at different angles. They all seemed very happy though.

"Hi, umm, I'm Sebastian!" he began. "Are all of you electrons?"

A cacophonous chatter ensued as the electrons began introducing themselves all at once.

"How do you know about electrons?" Ellie inquired.

"Yeah, how do you know about us?"

"Well, I'm not from the Quantum Realm, but I have been on a journey through the layers. My guide, Philly the Photon, told me about electrons. Where am I?"

"You are in a positive charged electron cloud. How do you feel?"

"I feel positively charged," Sebastian quipped and chuckled.

All of sudden Wiki came bouncing and waving through the group of electrons. They were scattered like bowling pins and everyone erupted in laughter as they flew through the air. As they returned to their orbit around Sebastian, it looked as if bright particles of light were emitted from each of them along a wave.

That was interesting, he thought and made a mental note to think about that later.

His merriment was short-lived though as he began to contemplate why and how he ended up there. A bit of guilt and disappointment arose within him as he remembered what had happened.

"I was traveling with my companions through the Electron Sea when Wiki and I became separated from them. The tunnel collapsed around us and it was my fault."

The orbiting electrons all started talking at once. He could not understand anything, but a word here and there. It sounded as if they were all expressing empathy and wanted to offer advice.

"You know, Sebastian," the electron that Ellie referred to as Auntie began speaking, "learning to navigate the Quantum Realm is difficult for all of us. Electrons have more freedom than other particles and waves, but even we cannot cross certain barriers and layers. You are not from here, and yet you have made it this far. Do not feel guilty for trying. You are never guaranteed success. Mistakes and failures will always occur before you are successful. However, if you reexamine the patterns and learn what it is that you did wrong, then you will become wiser and make fewer mistakes. Don't be afraid of making mistakes and experiencing failures."

Sebastian listened to what she said and he understood.

"Believe in yourself and have confidence in your ability to learn. If you do not know how to overcome an obstacle, then look for the knowledge and tools that are needed. You can always learn what is required if you believe that you can. Now, how can we assist you on your journey?"

Sebastian felt much better after listening to Auntie.

She seems very wise. Alright, I will try to believe in myself then. I hope that they can help.

"I am on a journey to find the Lair of Grunk the Great Graviton."

"Ooooooo! That's a dangerous path."

"Hmm. That's a difficult journey!" said another.

"No one goes there. They never return."

"You must travel through the negative charged electron cloud and then into the Abyss of Emptiness. The Abyss will attempt to steal your mind and soul. It is a very dangerous place," Auntie informed him.

They were scaring Sebastian. He stood there for several moments contemplating what he should do.

I don't want to go. This isn't fair.

He thought about the questions that he needed to be answered. Grunk was the only one who could get him home again. He also thought about the fear and what Auntie had said to him.

I'm tired of being afraid. Courage, I must have the courage.

"Why do you want to go there?" Ellie asked.

"I must go. I need to understand light and energy, I need to understand its power, and I need to find a way back to my home and my parents. Philly the Photon said that Grunk is the only one who can provide the answers."

"Hmm. Maybe. Maybe. You must be very strong! Ok, we will help you."

The electrons were concerned for Sebastian, but believed that he had the potential to find his way.

"Sebastian," Ellie began in a caring voice, "you are in a positive charged electron cloud. In order to reach Grunk's lair, you will need to travel through the negative charged electron cloud and the Abyss of Emptiness. Both will challenge you in ways you cannot know."

"I know, Ellie. I feel as if I have already been pushed to my limits. I have lost my friends, Philly and Viki, and I am exhausted. However, I must find Grunk's lair or I can't return home. I have no choice. I have to go."

"Okay, I see. I understand. I will show you! Come on then. Let's go and we will prepare for the rest of your journey."

Ellie, Sebastian, and Wiki said their goodbyes and thanks to the other electrons and then turned toward an alleyway.

"Sebastian, there is a trick to making it through the negative electron cloud. The electrons that reside in the negative charged cloud, we refer to them as Negatives, are innocent enough, but they will trap you in their negative way of thinking. The trick is to change the heart and mind of one electron. It will cause a ripple effect and result in a temporary positive charge."

"But how do I do that, Ellie?"

"Be the change. It may prove difficult, but you must have a positive impact on them if you are to make it out. Otherwise, you risk being trapped in their negativity for an eternity. Just be positive, think positive thoughts, and be happy. Smile at everyone and give everyone respect and the benefit of the doubt. Believe in yourself and your ability to bring happiness to those around you. Above all else, do not judge them," Ellie clarified with a big, warm smile.

What does judging them have to do with anything? I'm not even sure what that means. Oh well, I suppose I'll figure it out.

"When the flip occurs, it will happen very fast and the positive charge will create a domino effect. There are too many negatives to overcome for long, and they will all flip back, including you, if you don't escape."

"What do I do when this happens?" Sebastian asked.

"You must utilize the change in the directional flow of electrons. Ride the wave of change! Every negative electron that comes in contact with the positive electron will be affected."

Sebastian thought that this might be easy for him. He was consistently conquering his fear and was becoming more confident by the moment.

He then remembered something. "What is the Abyss of Emptiness?"

"We have a legend about the Abyss of Emptiness. However, it is not for you to know our legends. You must write your own legend. You will need all your power, knowledge, and wisdom to overcome what lies ahead. I will not see you again on this journey. I like you, Sebastian. I know you will make it to Grunk the Great Graviton. He will get you back home. Here, have a charge!" Ellie tickled Sebastian, and then kissed him on the cheek.

"Good luck!"

She quickly opened the portal in the alley. Wiki looked at Sebastian with giant, happy eyes, jumped into his arms and licked his face. He realized that Wiki was not going with him.

"Goodbye, Wiki the Wave. Please tell Viki that I am grateful for her guidance. Tell her how beautiful she is. Goodbye, Nancy. Thank you."

Sebastian wiped the tears from his eyes, mustered his courage, and then dove into the portal.

Chapter 11
NEGATIVE NANCY THE ELECTRON

Sebastian instantly felt like his energy level dropped. His body was heavy and his mind seemed thick like it was wading through mud.

Sebastian had a bit of trouble adjusting to this environment. It was another bubble, but the sky was dark. He saw the electrons that he expected, but their blue light was very dim.

"Who are you? What are you doing here? You don't belong here!"

Sebastian whirled around to see an electron glaring at him with a frown. He remembered what Ellie had said to him, and he instantly smiled as big and friendly a smile as he possibly could.

"Hello there! My name is Sebastian."

"Huh! What, uhh, well, my name is Nancy. Some call me Negative Nancy—I have a down spin. You're in a negative charged electron cloud. Uhh, you're ugly! What are you? Oh, wait! You're a human, right?"

"Why yes, I am. I come from a place called Earth. It's a beautiful place with all sorts of different people and cultures," Sebastian said with a big, happy smile and a light laugh.

"I've made a few friends on my journey. I really enjoyed the electrons in the positive electron cloud."

"What? The Positives? Oh no, those guys are weird. They float around all happy and stuff. They act as if they are better than us. We don't like positives around here. We don't like anyone that is different. To think of it, I don't even like any of the electrons here either," Nancy replied as she curled her lip.

Sebastian felt the negative vibes from being around Negative Nancy. He understood what Ellie explained to him now.

Well, how can I make her life a little better? I know!

"Hey, Nancy! Do you have any pets?"

"Pets? Pets? Goodness, no. Pets are messy, they stink and they are always making noise. Uck! No, no pets!"

Eh! That didn't work.

"I've been on a long journey. I've been traveling through the Quantum Realm. It's my first trip to your realm. It's amazing! I've learned so much and made some wonderful friends," he said in an attempt to strike up a positive conversation.

"Yada, yada, yada! What are you doing here! Come on! Come on! I'm taking you to the council."

Nancy was proving to be a bit difficult.

Nancy has a bad attitude and she's not nice. Look at the way she talks with that frown. She looks mean and I bet the council is just as mean. I don't like her.

Sebastian suddenly noticed the change in his attitude.

She is affecting me and is definitely too negative to be around.

"Debbi! Debbi! Look what I found," Nancy cried in a disgusted voice. Then she leaned over to Sebastian and said, "She smells really bad. They call her Debbi Downer! Nobody likes her."

"Ech! He's so ugly! What is it?" Debbi Downer questioned. "Whatever it is, it doesn't belong here. Let's give him a charge!"

Sebastian was in trouble. He did not think that their charge was the same as those of positive electrons. He was starting to have a really bad opinion about these negative electrons.

What can I do?

He was getting angry and frustrated. Sebastian was tired, and all he wanted to do was to lie down and rest.

These negative electrons are taking all of my energy.

The council room was flooding with negative electrons. Everybody wanted to see this ugly human. They were hoping for an opportunity to *charge* him.

There were thousands, and they all fell into orbits around him.

He realized that this was his chance. He had to come up with a way to make Nancy smile. He was not being thoughtful and was starting to judge everyone. He had to stop the negative thought pattern, and the best way do that was to be thankful. He quickly began thinking about some things that he was thankful for.

I'm thankful for my new friends: Philly, Viki, Wiki, and Ellie. I'm thankful that I have parents that love and protect me; many children do not know what that's like. I'm really thankful for them. I'm thankful for my dog, Einstein; boy, what a comfort he has been to me and oh, how much fun we've shared.

A soft and happy smile crept across his face.

He thought about Nancy, realized that she is a product of her environment, and probably wanted to be happy. He believed that she might have experienced a lot of rejection and meanness in her life.

He turned towards Negative Nancy with a soft smile and said, "Nancy, I am normally a happy person. Being here has been difficult. I don't feel very happy right now. So, I was thinking of something that makes me feel better is doing something nice for someone else."

Sebastian closed his eyes and focused.

If I don't make it out of here, then I will at least attempt one last positive deed. I will then have no regrets.

Nancy looked at him slightly confused. *Sebastian is kind of nice,* she realized.

Sebastian reached into his pocket and pulled out a beautiful bright yellow Gerbera Daisy. "This is for you!"

Nancy gazed upon the amazing flower. Her face softened and a big, thankful smile crept across her face.

"Thank you, Sebastian. Thank you," she said softly.

It all happened so quickly that Sebastian was startled. Nancy began glowing brightly and she started spinning upwards. The positive charge spread and all the electrons started glowing just like Nancy. Ten, then twenty, then forty, and then the whole bubble lit up with a spectacular neon blue glow.

Then he saw it.

"Is that the portal to the Abyss, Nancy?"

She looked in the direction he pointed.

"Yes, it is."

"I need to get there right now. Can you help me?"

Nancy looked at him and said, "You have made me smile. I had forgotten what it feels like. Thank you and I will help you willingly."

She took his hand and glowed brighter than all the other electrons. They all moved and cleared the way forward.

"Feel the wave. It is flowing very strongly."

Sebastian felt it and embraced the wave frequency. By the time they reached the portal, the blue light was fading. The electrons were returning to their negative state. It reminded him of how the electron tunnel collapsed.

"Shine as brightly as you can, Nancy. You can influence them to be positive and happy. I believe in you. Be nice to them." Sebastian smiled and kissed her cheek. "Thank you, Nancy."

Before she could say a word, he dove through the portal. The electrons had all lost their bright glows; all of them, except for Nancy. She remained there for some time, just looking upon her beautiful flower and whispered to herself, "I will hold onto this happiness for as long as I can. Thank you, Sebastian."

Chapter 12
THE ABYSS OF EMPTINESS

Sebastian was floating in the darkness. There was nothing: no light, no sound, and no sensation on his skin. There wasn't any sense of temperature, and there wasn't a single *vibration* except those coming from within his brain and body.

The Abyss of Emptiness. This place is very uncomfortable.

It was completely empty. At first, Sebastian was fine. He just relaxed as he floated around and enjoyed the silence. He was unaware of what direction he was moving, or if he was moving at all. His mind wandered.

What am I doing here?

Sebastian began to question himself.

I don't belong here. I barely survived this journey thus far, and I caused everyone so much grief. I couldn't hold my focus with Wiki and I caused us to be separated from my friends. Oh, goodness, Viki is probably so upset and disappointed with me. Her heart must be broken to have lost Wiki. I can't believe I messed up so badly.

Sebastian began to feel a deep pain in his heart and stomach.

I hope Ellie will help Wiki find Viki.

Sebastian was feeling sad and guilty.

That was just the beginning.

How long have I been here? I feel so lost. I don't know what I'm doing here. Why didn't I just go home? I might never make it home now.

Sebastian began crying in a flood of painful memories and regrets.

I just want to go home! I just want to go home, he cried to himself.

Sebastian spent quite a bit of time and energy being lost in this state. He was beginning to feel like he was the worst person alive and that no one would ever forgive him for all his mistakes. He believed that his father was so disappointed in him.

I feel so lost, so very lost.

Sebastian began thinking about the first time that he had met Philly the Photon, the light particle. He was so fun and friendly.

"Wait a moment!" Sebastian exclaimed, and then he realized what was happening.

"This is the Abyss of Emptiness! The Abyss of Emptiness!" he repeated aloud.

This place makes me feel so empty and alone. I must find the strength to overcome the negative thoughts. They are destroying my confidence and my hope for returning home.

Sebastian tightened his jaw and looked deep within himself.

I am a good and decent boy. I care about my Mom and Dad. I care about others and I want them to be happy. I'm not perfect, but I work hard and try to do the right thing. I know that I have the courage and strength to make it home.

Sebastian changed his whole attitude and perspective with those simple thoughts and began to think about all the things that he was grateful for on this journey.

Sebastian smiled.

Dear ol' Philly! What a squirrelly particle he is. I hope that I get to see him again. I'm going to give him a big hug.

Philly had helped him to overcome his fears and believe in his abilities. The ability to understand and recognize fear made Sebastian feel like he had so much more control over himself. Understanding the concept of becoming aware was so powerful. It had just helped him overcome his own negative thinking.

He was thankful for his newfound courage and how it increased his confidence. It enabled him to learn and do new things.

Learning about Viki and how she communicated with vibrations was so cool and different from how Sebastian communicated, and yet in a way it was the same.

I wonder if there are different ways to communicate with people who look or act differently than I do. Hmm. I seem to remember that Mom and Dad have some books on personalities and communication styles. I should look at them.

He thought about how all things, even animals, are complex enclosed systems of vibrations, which are waves and particles. *Vibrations are the language of the universe,* he recalled Viki vibrating.

He thought about how fond he was of Wiki the Wave.

He was so snuggly. Viki could alternate her frequencies, but Wiki could alternate both his frequency and amplitude. So cool!

Wiki had helped him visualize how vibrations travel in waves and particles across the universe. He learned that the movement between two or more particles or forces creates vibrations. The vibrations have predictable repeating patterns that are organized by their frequencies. The amount of power and force that a frequency has is measured by its amplitude.

Hmm. Do humans attract others based upon the similarities in their frequencies? I've noticed how certain people usually attract others who act, dress, and think like themselves. If so, does that mean that they also repel others with different frequencies? I bet being aware of this pattern in my behavior will help me be more mindful of how I interact with people who are different from me. I have so many questions.

He thought about how Ellie was so positive. Just being around her made him happy and feel encouraged.

Those positive charged electrons were all so helpful and caring.

Sebastian recalled the change in Negative Nancy. He positively influenced her life simply by doing something nice.

I will never forget how a simple act of kindness can affect someone so much. That act also made me feel good about the kind of person I am. Out of all the things that I've learned on this journey, I am most grateful for this truth.

I see how my behaviors may affect others. I want to make others feel good and be inspired. If I have a positive attitude, which reflects my perspective, then I will be able to have a positive effect on them. I don't know how to have a positive attitude all the time, but from now on, I will try to be aware of how my actions affect others. I bet being more positive will also attract good things and good people into my life.

Sebastian recalled that his father had a book called *The Power of Positive Thinking*.

I have overheard Dad encouraging several of his friends to read it. I need to look at it, but I think I get how it works.

Sebastian began to relax. He drifted in the darkness for so long that he began to lose any sense of his body. His mind began to expand into the darkness. He felt at peace and as if he was not only a part of the universe, but one with it.

Chapter 13

GRUNK THE GREAT GRAVITON

Something strange is happening to me.

As he allowed his mind to merge with the darkness, he felt an equal increase in what he could only describe as *love*.

Yes, I feel so much love. This is absolutely amazing! Sebastian became aware of the slow, beautiful waves of love seeping into every part of his body and mind.

My mind is flooded with the color red. I wonder if the colors in the rainbow are light frequencies, then maybe different emotions are made of the same light frequencies. I guess since atoms make up the molecules that are emotions, and atoms have frequencies too, that seeing colors while experiencing emotions would normal. Hmm, Sebastian pondered, *this feeling of love must be some specific type of frequency.*

So many questions. So much to learn. So much to understand. This journey has showed me so much. It seems like the more I learn, the more I realize how much I need to learn.

"BOOOOMMM!"

Suddenly a powerful pulse rippled through the darkness. It tore through Sebastian and it felt as if he was about to explode with ecstasy.

Then the words came. It was a deep slow wave, but it was very powerful.

"WHO HAS DARED TO ENTER MY LAIR?" a voice deeply boomed inside his mind. "Most do not survive the journey through the Abyss. DO YOU KNOW WHO I AM?" the voice rumbled intimidatingly.

Sebastian was not afraid. He listened and felt the overwhelming power of this being. He felt his own power rise up within, and he responded confidently. He spoke boldly, but with respect.

"I believe you to be Grunk the Great Graviton."

There came a slow deep rumbling laugh. "Yes, I guess that is what they call me in the Outer Realms."

Grunk sensed the power and greatness of this young man. Sebastian would grow into a tremendous force for good and a seeker of knowledge. Grunk knew that sharing his wisdom with Sebastian would not be wasted. He had truly earned the right to be here.

"I AM A GRAVITON!" roared the greatest graviton of them all.

"I AM AN EPICENTER OF GREAT ATTRACTIVE FORCE."

Sebastian felt the force of Grunk's words.

"What exactly is a graviton?" Sebastian inquired.

"I am a quantum particle: a special type of particle, similar to Philly. I carry one of the four fundamental forces of the universe."

"Force? Yes, I remember Philly mentioning four universal forces. What exactly is a force?"

"Good question. A force is something that can change the motion of something else. For instance, if a bat is swung at a ball and *forces* it to go in a different direction, then this action is a result of one or more fundamental forces. Can you give me an example of another type of action that represents a force?"

"Most definitely. Whenever I jump, I am always sucked back down to the ground."

"Very nice. Thus is the force that I carry—gravity. All four forces have a specific strength at both close and far distances. I have the weakest strength of the four at the shortest distances. In quantum, I am a rather insignificant player. However, I have the greatest strength over long distances. For example, the Sun's gravity pulls all the planets, including earth, towards its center. Gravity keeps all the planets in orbit around the Sun. On Earth, all things are drawn towards its center by gravity. Gravitons vary in size. They form tubes or spheres and are the energy carriers of the force of gravity. We are invisible, but gravity is at the foundation of all life and all matter. Without the perfect amount of gravity, you would not exist."

Sebastian's mind was churning with questions. So much so that he was lost in his own thoughts for quite some time.

Chapter 14
THE TRUTH SEEKER

"WHY HAVE YOU COME?" boomed the Great Graviton.

Sebastian was a little startled at first. He had been so lost in his own thoughts. "Grunk, I began this journey with the intent of learning about Photons and Light."

"Ahhhh," came Grunk's deep growl, "and have you obtained your knowledge?"

"I have obtained knowledge that has altered my perspective. It has changed who I am and what I will become. However, Philly the Photon shared only a little with me. Do you know Philly the Photon?"

"Yes, indeed I know Philly. Philly was born of vibrations in the outer layers of my realm. He is quite the character. Go on."

"You mentioned four fundamental forces. Philly mentioned them to me as well, but can you explain them?"

"Some time you must return to the Quantum Realm and journey to seek the knowledge of my siblings. The twins, Stumpy the Strong and Weirhorn the Weak, will be very difficult to find because they conceal themselves in matter. The fourth of us dominates your world. Tell me: what are the most vital resources to your civilization?"

"Well, energy, I guess."

"Ha! Energy comes in many forms. Energy is a word that describes the power of forces. Kinetic, potential, and radiant are primary energies derived from the four forces. There are various forms of these, including elastic and rest mass energy, heat and visible light, chemical and nuclear energy, and one more that is a product of the fourth force. What is it?

Sebastian suddenly realized, "Electricity. Everything around us is powered by electricity."

"Good, very good. The forces provide potential energy. Any type of energy must be able to be converted from one form of energy into another form of energy. Two primary forms of energy come from a single force. One is the electrical field. What is the other? What pairs with electricity to create an electrical motor?"

Sebastian recalled Philly mentioning something about the electromagnetic force, "Is it Magnetism?"

"Yes, indeed. You must return and explore the universe through Maggie Magnetism and her brother, Elmer the Electrical Current. *Electromagnetism* is the fourth force. Light, heat, electricity, and magnetism are some of the energies derived from electromagnetism."

"I don't understand. How is the light and heat from a fire the same as light and heat from electricity, or for that matter, from the sun?"

"Think, young Sebastian. What did your friends teach you? What did Viki, Wiki, and Philly teach you?"

Sebastian thought about all his experiences with his new friends: vibrations, waves, frequencies, photons, and electrons. He closed his eyes and tried to visualize something that could explain how all these things are the result of vibrational interactions.

Questions! I must ask questions. Specific questions.

"Vibration is a wave-like movement. Movement is relative between two or more objects. Can vibrations be defined as movement between two forces? For instance, between an electrical and a magnetic force?"

Grunk roared with laughter. "Yes, indeed it can. Keep going."

"Ok, so if the vibrations of the electromagnetic field move through time and space in waves, then I would assume that these waves would create something like a highway or transportation system across the universe. I learned that there are different types of wave patterns and they are referred to as frequencies. I wonder how many different frequencies are possible."

"That's a great question. Let's just say that all the different frequencies fall within the Electromagnetic Radiation Spectrum. At one end are radio and microwave frequencies that move towards visible light and on up to gamma rays."

"What a minute!" Sebastian's mind was thinking quickly now. "Radio waves? I can hear radio waves."

"Not quite, Sebastian. What is Philly?"

"A photon. A light particle. Hmm. Do particles travel via waves? At the speed of light?"

Grunk once again rumbled with admiration at how astute Sebastian was. "Yes. However, a *light* particle does not only refer to visible light frequencies. A photon is a *quanta*, a measurable unit, of light. *Light* refers to a particle, such as a photon, which travels on all frequencies of the Electromagnetic Radiation (EMR) Spectrum. Photons are a carrier particle of energetic force of electromagnetism."

"So, back to radio waves. Why can't I hear radio waves? I listen to the radio every day."

"Because radio waves are how you transport information. Radios receive radio waves and convert them into sound waves, which are different, yet similar, than light waves. Sound waves are a topic for another time."

"Okay, the next question then. Does the visible light spectrum refer to the colors of the rainbow?"

"Yes."

"Well, I know that microwaves heat my food. I know that fire produces light and heat. I know that Sunlight provides both light and heat. Does the Sun emit more than just the visible light spectrum?"

"Yes."

"Hmm. I know that lightning emits light in the form of photons, is electrical, has the ability to start fire, and is strong enough to rip apart trees. Are all of these a result of electrons that move along on an electromagnetic wave?"

"No, not exactly. Electrons are the energetic force carriers of electromagnetism. Photons are created from the electrons." Grunk rumbled.

"That's sort of confusing. So, let me reason this one out. Hmm. The different electromagnetic waves make up the Electromagnetic Radiation (EMR) spectrum. Is radiation the same as a wave?"

"Yes."

"Ok, then EMR is like a transportation highway of sorts for particles. Particles are made up of sphere-shaped systems of vibrations. Both electrons and photons are particles that travel on these waves. How do electrons create photons?"

"Think of it this way. Forces are carried by particles, which are spheres that have a specific frequency and influence the overall shape of their wave. They travel along the radiation highway, which has a different highway for each different frequency. Sometimes they intersect. Each particle is a result of multiple highways intersecting. The size of the force carrier, like an electron, is a result of the specific combination of highways converging at a single point. This creates a sphere. Interactions between electrons can create other wave patterns within its relative system. Photons can result from these interactions. Photons have a different set of characteristics and have a specific frequency wave that is similar to electrons, but different. Electrons can attract extra energy in the form of photons as they move around. Thus, photons can also be emitted from electrons as they move. One vibrational pattern can influence the creation of another vibrational pattern because everything is connected and shares the same basic frequencies."

"I get it. That makes more sense. So, the flow of electrons that split the sky open with lightning carries multiple forms of energy. Photons that have frequencies within the visible light spectrum are emitted and allow me to see light. Electrons create electrical current. They both have enough energetic force to convert one form of energy into another. Photons and other particles can vary in size and frequency patterns. These variations give rise to all the different forms of energy, such as light, fire, heat, and electricity. Am I correct?"

"Yes, indeed. It is a bit more complex than your explanation, but that is the general idea."

"Grunk, when I was floating around prior to meeting you, I experienced an immense feeling of love. At the same time, my mind was flooded with the color red. Do my emotions reflect underlying frequency patterns?"

"Wow! How astute of you. Well, are you aware of the sequence in which humans develop from particles and forces?"

"I think so. Philly told me about particles and forces interacting to create atoms, then molecules, then cells, etc."

"Correct. Imagine a thread of photons and electrons flowing through the center of every atom. There are different types of atoms: hydrogen, oxygen, carbon, sodium, etc. This thread has a specific frequency and affects the frequency pattern of all the atoms that it connects. Each atom has its own frequency pattern, which is originally derived from a combination of EMR patterns. Different atoms combine and form molecules. This is another level of new frequency pattern combinations. Human emotions are simply molecules that are created by your body and are released into other parts of your body. Their creation is a result of a trigger frequency. They also act as a trigger frequency for other molecules in your body. Humans are composed of specific atom combinations. Each atom shares a part of the continuous system of threads and has a specific range of frequency patterns. Don't forget, frequency patterns are simply a continuous system of waves. Emotions are nothing more than a molecule. Molecules have frequency patterns that are interacting with other molecules. Emotions have substance. Emotions are a specific frequency pattern."

"That makes so much sense. So, emotions and feelings are derived from the basic frequencies that are represented on the EMR Spectrum. Love—the emotion, is a frequency pattern."

"Well done. Yes, love is a universal language because all humans share the basic frequency. That frequency is so basic that it can be triggered, and its amplitude increased, at multiple levels of molecular structures. However, it is only one of many emotional frequencies. Hate, anger and guilt are others. Some emotions improve one's quality of life, while others destroy it. This effect is very physical, not simply metaphorical. The frequency patterns in one's body can destroy and disrupt other healthy frequency patterns, or they can nurture and sustain them. There are also combinations and variations of emotional frequency patterns. Have you ever experienced conflicting emotions? Or have you ever heard a song that overwhelmed you with an emotion. Maybe it made you cry."

"Yes, I have. In fact, I have on this journey."

"Be aware, Sebastian. People that are aware of these patterns use their knowledge to manipulate others. Some do so for good, like someone that inspires you. Others use their knowledge to the detriment of others, for their own personal selfishness and greed, which is another frequency pattern. Learn to recognize these emotional frequency patterns in both yourself and in others: love, compassion, empathy, fear, guilt, sadness, anger, and greed. You can use your knowledge of these to attract and inspire, enslave and control, or repel and remove others. Be mindful of your actions, your choices, and how you affect others."

Sebastian was deep in thought and tried to process all that Grunk was conveying. Grunk was astonished at the intensity in which he was learning and engaged.

"Everything that you experience is a result of your relative frequency patterns. The ones that operate within the relative system of your own body as well as the frequency patterns that you interact with coming from your external environment. These interacting frequency patterns trigger action and reaction changes in their sequences."

"Everything is starting to make sense. My overall frequency patterns affect everyone and everything in my environment. Everything is connected by the threads of EMR frequencies and particles. They form a continuum of movement and interactions. Wow. So cool."

"Very well done, Sebastian. Very well done, indeed. Your thought process is brilliant. You have proven yourself capable of critical thinking, deductive reasoning, and overcoming your fears. You now have the tools to discover the truths of yourself and of the universe. You have proven yourself worthy of the knowledge from the Quantum Realm."

Sebastian's mind raced with many thoughts and insights. He was thankful to have earned Grunk's approval and to have received his wisdom.

Chapter 15

A PATH TO ENLIGHTENMENT

"Sebastian," Grunk began, "science is a field that seeks truth through experiments and observations. Questions must be asked in expectation of receiving a specific answer. The answer will lead one down a path to more questions."

"Hmm," Sebastian was brought back from his reverie, "what happens if I ask a question based upon a wrong assumption?"

"Good question. There is a process used called the *Scientific Method*."

"I heard about that before. Dad spoke to me about the Scientific Method the night that I entered the Quantum Realm."

"Good. Take this opportunity to understand it a little better. Repetition is the key to learning. The Scientific Method is the method wherein one who is inquiring automatically assumes that the information attained will be erroneous, false and incomplete or inaccurate. Thus, one will purposely test, criticize, correct, retest, and improve the overall accuracy and completeness of a belief or system of beliefs."

"Wow! That seems like a good way to confirm if something is true or not."

"I agree. The general process is: 1) ask a question, 2) propose an hypothesis—make an assumption based upon preexisting information, 3) conduct experiments, 4) make observations of the results, and 5) repeat and retest for consistency."

"Hmm. That process definitely seems like I could apply it to both scientific and self-discovery experiments."

"Yes! Analyzing your own behavior and how it affects everyone in your environment by using impersonal logic is a great baseline for understanding one's self; it is incomplete, yet a great start," grumbled Grunk.

"Grunk, if I believe something, based upon my own personal set of experiences, then it seems like everyone else would develop their own beliefs in the same way. If different people have different experiences, then it would make sense that a few people would probably have similar experiences. However, it seems like the majority of people would have completely different experiences, and thus, different conclusions and assumptions. Does sharing the same belief with others make it true?"

Grunk rumbled with amusement at the depth of insight from this boy.

"That is a complicated question. Indeed, entire generations of humans believed that the Earth was flat. For thousands of years, people were discouraged to challenge what they were told to believe and not to ask questions. People are still influenced in this manner in many places. It was a bit more than one hundred years ago that humans believed in slavery; it was accepted as god ordained and moral by many. Even in your world today, some believe it is morally okay to require a being to submit to another's will through some form of force, coercion, or manipulation. Have you ever known a *bully*?"

"Oh yeah. I know a few."

"Slavery still exists in many forms. However, time forces all things to change. When you acquire new knowledge, you must accept the responsibility that it requires. Truths, morals, and beliefs are all relative based upon the common acceptance of said beliefs. Some beliefs vary from community to community. Other beliefs permeate large numbers of people that span across cultures and countries. These relative systems vary in size and shape. Does this resemble any of the patterns that you have discovered in the Quantum Realm?"

"Hmm. Yes, I think so. Everything down here seems to be determined by its surroundings. We tend to have the greatest effect on those things in our closest proximity. Wait! That sounds like the concept of Relativity."

"Indeed it is. The understanding of quantum mechanic processes is the unifying truth of everything, every being, and every life form in the universe. The patterns that originate here, in the Quantum Realm, give rise to every diverse and varied pattern in your everyday life. This applies to belief systems, social and economic structures, and the cycles of all life forms. It is all connected by the connected system of vibrations—the space-time continuum. The scientists in your world are still discovering new patterns and how everything is connected, so you must be willing to change your beliefs when new information modifies an existing assumption of truth. These new truths take time to travel from person to person. They will then choose whether to accept them as true and some will not."

"Well, how do I know if what I believe or assume is correct, or right, or truth?" Sebastian asked.

"Ahhhh, yes, that is a good question. Now, this is the strength of Science. You must try to find the answers over and over again. Look for the patterns to repeat everywhere, and then discover how they are all connected. Others must find those same patterns. Most importantly, the answers and assumptions must fit into a larger puzzle of truth. Everything is connected and everything must have a connection to everything else," Grunk rumbled with gravity.

"If truth is relative, then how do I treat others who don't have my knowledge or that believe differently?"

"Always try to do the right thing, Sebastian, for yourself, for others, and for the environment that sustains your life. Try to have a net positive impact on your realm of influence. Sometimes you will be unable to. Sometimes doing what's right for yourself will conflict with doing what's right for others or the environment. Learn from those experiences and keep trying to do what you believe is right. However, continue to allow yourself to be challenged by different perspectives of truth and insight, both in your scientific explorations and in your personal life. Don't be afraid of being proved wrong."

Sebastian recalled some of the instances in which he had been corrected by his parents, by his teachers, and by his coaches. He didn't like being corrected.

I think I will need to work on my perspective and learn how to appreciate and honestly evaluate what they say to me.

"You are on the right path, Sebastian. Our time together is ending. Have you obtained the knowledge and courage that you sought?"

"Yes, and so much more. I remember hearing or reading this before:

knowledge is power. I feel so empowered and confident. Thank you, Grunk. You have earned my respect."

"Ahh, you have also earned mine. Believe in yourself; believe in your dreams and ideas. The more that you believe in them, the more people will believe in you and the larger your *realm of influence* will become. If there is truth in your ideas and beliefs, then you will find that others will also be able to confirm them. Seek those who see things differently than you; they will provide alternative perspectives and other ways to understand science and life. Don't be fearful of people's differences; they are different for a reason. Listen and learn what those reasons are without judging them; listen to their stories. See life through their eyes before you make presumptions. The more one experiences, the more complete the set of perspectives. You will also have a greater realm of understanding and influence, and you will become wiser. Be honest with yourself and change when one of your assumptions is proven wrong or to be an incomplete truth."

"Yes, Grunk, I will own my mistakes and will not be afraid to admit when I am wrong. I will modify my beliefs as I learn new perspectives of truth and new discoveries of science. I will not defend my ideas for the sake of my pride or for being right," Sebastian said humbly.

Grunk continued with his final rumblings, "A single idea, a single truth can change the world. Find a way to share what you discover, young Sebastian. Believe in yourself! Believe that *good* people deserve to change the world with their ideas, not the greedy and selfish ones. Use your understanding of *science, courage,* and *love* to make a *positive* impact. Be the change that inspires the world and share the awesomeness of science. Your Father will be very proud of you. You have proven yourself worthy."

Grunk the Great Graviton rumbled no more.

Chapter 16
THE JOURNEY HOME BEGINS

Sebastian once again was left floating in a sea of darkness and silence. His brain was hurting like it was being squished by two giant hands. He ceased trying to control his thoughts so that it was free to flow into the stillness of his surroundings.

There was a slow distant vibration starting to softly hum. Sebastian opened his eyes. Sparkling lights were forming in the outer realms of the great sphere he, apparently, was centered in.

The humming increased, and the number of bright sparkling lights increased too. More and more lights flashed into existence as they moved faster and faster around the outer realms. They started forming great rivers around the outside. Sebastian was feeling the pull of gravity move him from the center towards the area of greatest movement.

In a flash, a river of light burst into the inner realms. A funnel formed, like a lightning hurricane, and it changed the humming into a great roaring. It was moving toward the center of the sphere. The substance that Sebastian was floating in began to move and lights popped into existence all throughout. The darkness disappeared and everything within the sphere was raging in perfect harmony.

The hurricane of light grew larger and larger towards the center. As it grew, Sebastian was pulled harder and faster towards the bottom tip of the great light hurricane.

Soon the light will rip me to pieces!

"No, it will not!" he said contradicting his initial thoughts. "I will harness its power and ride it all the way home."

Whooosh!

In an instant, Sebastian was swept away into the beautiful pattern of light that flowed like a long twisting snake. Smaller patterns of light began to form and swirl around inside the tremendous hurricane.

Sebastian held on to his focus with all his might. He closed his eyes, centered himself, and concentrated his thoughts. He merged his mind into the flow of vibrations around him. Then he set his intent on Philly and home. Suddenly, the entire hurricane of light began to sway and buckle under his will. In a great and powerful motion, the hurricane tunnel completely changed its direction.

He could now see through the light tunnel to the outside of the sphere. Sebastian moved with the speed of a photon, and his face rippled from the force of gravity. His spirit soared, and he flew with the might of the Great Graviton.

"I will miss this place. This magical Quantum Realm!"

Chapter 17
THE PATH TO LIGHT

Sebastian flew through the portal and exited the giant sphere. He was now floating high above it. He looked at the amazing spectacle of swirling white and neon blue light. He would never forget how it moved and felt.

The giant sphere seized and convulsed. In a single moment, all of the light waves were sucked tightly into the center. Then it exploded in an even burst pushing outward towards the outer realms of the giant sphere. The light dissipated across the outer layer in sizzling flames, and then it all disappeared back into total darkness.

Sebastian looked around, and he could see the same tiny, bright speckles of light that appeared when he first met Philly the Photon. Then, off in the distance, he saw a tiny light that was moving very fast. It left a long wavy trail of light like a shooting star. The light was racing straight for him and was growing in size.

Zwoomp!

It was Philly!

"Hellllllloooooooo, Sebastian!" Philly howled as he came to a halt directly in front him.

"Hello Philly! It's great to see you. I thought that I would never have a chance to thank you for my amazing experience, for the adventure of a lifetime through the Quantum Realm. I want to thank you for the amazing particle friends that I made, the tremendous journey of self-discovery, and the knowledge and wisdom of the Great Graviton. It was an absolutely life-changing adventure!"

"Yes, yes. You're welcome. You did very well. So, you met Grunk, did you?" Philly asked with enthusiastic interest.

"Yes, I sure did. I learned so much, Philly."

"I bet! What did you learn?"

"I learned that everything in the universe has a *pattern*. Patterns are created by movement between *forces* or *particles*. The collection of these movements are called vibrations. Vibrations move in a wave-like motion and flow throughout the entire universe. When vibrational waves intersect, they can form measurable spheres called particles. Particles carry forces of different types of energy patterns."

"What about me? What about photons?"

"Photons are particles too, and so are electrons. The waves that particles move along are part of the (EMR) Spectrum. Radiation refers to frequency waves. The spectrum refers to the different types of waves."

"What makes one wave different from another?"

Philly was enjoying the dialogue.

"The frequency! The frequency refers to the number of peaks within a given period of time or distance and is determined by its wavelength. The wavelength is the distance between peaks."

"Can you alter the strength of the frequency?"

"Hmm. I think so. I recall that the distance between the peak and the valley is called the amplitude. A specific frequency's amplitude can increase or decrease."

"What else? What else? What about light?"

"Well, if I remember correctly, light refers to two different things. Light is another word for photon. However, photons are energetic force carriers that move along the entire EMR Spectrum. There are many different frequencies; however, humans can only see a small segment of the spectrum and the photons that travel along those frequencies. This segment is called the visible light spectrum. A rainbow's colors are an example of the frequencies in the visible light spectrum. However, there are a large number of other electromagnetic wave frequencies too, like microwaves and radio waves."

"Can particles combine to make larger objects?"

"Yes. Particles carry a charge and attract other particles. They bump into one another and create subsystems of increasingly complex vibrations. The complex systems of vibrational movement through the space-time continuum give rise to things like photons, electrons, atoms, molecules, cells, humans, planets, and solar systems."

"Do humans detect electromagnetic waves?"

"Yes. We use eyes to see frequencies of light. We use our ears to hear frequencies of sound. Sound frequency waves are different from frequencies along the EMR Spectrum, but I haven't learned about that yet. We use our nose to smell different patterns of movement in the air. We use our vocal chords to produce sound frequencies. In addition, our skin can detect, absorb, and emit the changes in movement and temperature within our relative environment. These are essentially the changes occurring in the frequency patterns around us."

"Relativity. What did I share with you regarding time and relativity?"

"Well, a good way to measure time is to measure the movement patterns of two related objects. We can measure time by the orbit cycles of electrons around a nucleus of an atom, or like how we can measure years by how long it takes the Earth to orbit the Sun. This is called *relativity*."

"Does relativity apply to other concepts?"

"Yes. Everything is *relative* to what it is being compared to. Patterns move *relative* to one another. I can compare two different balls. If I were asked which one is bigger, I would observe and compare the only two options available. One ball is bigger compared to the other. As you can see, everything is relative. Everything we do, say or think affects everyone and everything in our environment, whether we observe it or not. The same words or act can generate a different reaction from two different people. Recognizing these relative patterns produces awareness. Once we become aware of something, we can then influence its change, and everything is always changing and moving."

"Right, right. What else?" Philly beamed with anticipation.

"Our level of awareness provides us with our unique *perspective*. Our perspective is relative, so it is always limited. Thus, it is important to get to know people who have different perspectives, different lives, different styles, and different beliefs from our *relative normal*. This can be uncomfortable, but it allows us to see life from someone else's perspective."

"How can you experience someone else's perspective?" Philly inquired.

"I learned that if I wish to understand something or someone's perspective, then I must experience it. I believe Dad always says, 'Don't judge someone until you have walked a mile in their shoes.' I must also listen and ask questions in order to fully understand their reasoning. I must hear their reasons without presumptions. Even if I don't agree with them or share their perspective, I can learn from them. They are a culmination of a lifetime of relative frequency patterns that they have experienced in their relative environments. I can never truly understand their continuum and what their lives are like. So, I must be willing to alter my beliefs and assumptions when I listen and the facts prove contrary."

"Very good. However, how does perspective apply to science?"

"Well, it applies to scientific analysis. Viewing an object, an experiment, etc., from multiple perspectives and angles, will enable us to have a more complete understanding. Discussing observations with different people who see things differently will also allow me to include their perspective into my broader understanding."

"Very good. Very good. Did you learn anything about fear, about courage, and about yourself?"

"Yes, indeed. Fear is extremely powerful. It can influence every decision I make, every thought that I have about myself, and even affects how I perceive others. Fear is only meant to provide caution and offer a moment for *reasoning*. However, my fear should not be the reason that I do or don't do something, unless, of course, I am in immediate danger."

"What causes fear?" Philly interjected.

"Fear is a reflection of a lack of *confidence* in what I think I can or cannot do, what I do not know, or what I do not understand. My fears are usually the result of inaccurate or inadequate information. This includes my awareness of others, my environment and the perspective that I have about my own abilities."

"How can you overcome fear?"

"I can use *courage* to disrupt my fear so that I can *reason* through the beliefs that cause me to have fear. This will allow me the opportunity to make logical and rational decisions. I can also seek knowledge to provide me with additional confidence to face the unknown. My Dad says, 'knowledge is power,' but I think someone more famous said that."

"Yes, I am familiar with that quote. Many people believe it to be true. One must place limits on the value of *power*. The pursuit of power can destroy you and those around you."

"Is the opposite true as well? If I don't have enough power over my own life, can someone else have enough power to destroy my life?"

"Yes, Yes. We must always pursue balance."

Sebastian paused a moment to reflect on his views on power and on how much right he had to control other people's lives to serve his own purposes.

"You were saying?" Philly redirected him back to the conversation.

"Well, having awareness and knowledge allows me to use my mind as a *tool*. The process of learning how to use these tools, both independently and in combination with other tools, is how I develop *wisdom*. It's like learning to use a saw, hammer, and screwdriver, and then using all of them to build a table."

Sebastian paused for a moment as he thought about all the things he had built with his father. It made him smile and then he continued.

"Recognizing patterns is the beginning of all intelligent life. Being able to understand basic patterns allows us to use them to understand increasingly more complex patterns."

"Have you been able to apply that on yourself?"

"Yes. I have learned to recognize the emotional patterns when I am feeling them, such as fear, courage, happiness, anxiety, and love. I have more control over them simply by being aware of when I experience them. I controlled my fear on this journey several times. Because I was self-aware of this emotion, I was able to alter it with courage.

"I also learned that the effect of a person's emotional patterns could have both a positive and a negative impact on themselves, others, and the environment."

"Indeed. Can you give me an example?"

"Yes, I sure can. I remember how nice Ellie was and how everyone loved her. She had a positive effect on others. She made people feel better. Negative Nancy was not nice and her attitude affected everyone negatively. Both effects are contagious. However, I also realized how a simple act of kindness could have a positive effect on others, like when I gave Nancy a flower. Making her feel good made me feel good too. I like that."

Philly jittered around and listened intently. "Sebastian, you have learned so much. Now let's see if you remember how to have fun."

Philly circled Sebastian, dodged forward and zapped him.

"Tag, you're it!"

"What, err, uh, hey!" A big smile spread across Sebastian's face.

"Game on!"

They flew off and chased each other at the speed of light. At the speed of Philly the Photon!

As Sebastian raced off, he knew that he would return home soon, but there was still so much more to learn. He promised to return someday to this world: the fantastical world of The Quantum Realm.

To be continued...

AUTHOR BIO

Mark A Montgomery lives in Oakland, California. In 2010, he experienced a life transforming psychotherapy process. The near instantaneous transformation inspired him to understand what had happened within his brain, and the flame was lit. He began an expedition into his own mind by researching psychology and biology, which led to neuroscience and chemistry and eventually, quantum physics. The journey produced an insatiable desire to understand the mysteries of the Quantum Realm. It was a healing process that turned into a passion for sharing quantum patterns with his son.

His passion led to the conviction that everyone would benefit from having a fundamental knowledge of how quantum patterns explain everything, but especially human behavior. Understanding quantum patterns can guide us in realizing truths about our environment, the nature of our existence, and our relationships. Every human experience is simply a collection of predictable moving vibrational patterns interacting within a continuum of the same. Learning to recognize these quantum patterns in human behavior can transform our lives.

Mark hopes that his writings will inspire you to see life as a series of net impacts on your environment, including people. Your thoughts affect your actions; your actions affect your environment; your environment affects your relative norm. Be inspired to have a net positive impact on all things.